Little Lu
Learns to Love

by Leah Vis

THREE HORSE
PUBLISHING

It was Saturday morning, and Little Lu had only one thing on her mind: brand-new paints.

She had the perfect day planned, and all she needed was blank sheets of paper, her painting supplies, and some cute little dollies to keep Baby Kady entertained.

Little Lu admired the rainbow-colored paints, and her heart felt like it would float up to the clouds. Surely birds were always outside, but at this moment they seemed to be singing just for her.

As Little Lu reached for her paintbrush, Mama announced,
"Cousin Henry is coming over in about fifteen minutes."

Little Lu felt like the birds outside suddenly stopped their song.
Cousin Henry definitely did *not* fit into her day of painting.

But she quickly recovered,
deciding that Cousin Henry
could just play with Baby Kady.

The birds continued to sing.
"Okay, Mama, I'll just lock the
door so Cousin Henry knows
not to come in."

"Oh no, Lu Lu. I would like you to help Cousin Henry feel welcome. Just
let him paint with you. I'm sure he would enjoy that."

Little Lu definitely did *not* want any help painting. He might mix the paint!
Or worse, he might waste the paint. Little Lu decided she needed to
solve this problem quickly, before the birds stopped singing altogether.

But before Little Lu could make a plan, she heard Mama talking at the front door. Suddenly, Cousin Henry raced over to Little Lu and gave her a huge bear hug.

"Lu Lu, I'm so happy to be here! I brought my best books and thought we could read them together. I can show you all my favorite pages. And then…"

"Ooooh," Little Lu was trying to sound interested. "But actually, you can just leave your books in the corner. I already have everything ready for a painting day. You like art, right?"

Cousin Henry's smile faded a bit but then grew again when he saw her table full of new, colorful paints.

"Noooo! Not there, Cousin Henry. *This* spot is perfect for you." She sat him down with a piece of paper and all the crayons he could ever need. Crayons would be good enough for him.

Now she could focus again.

The song of the birds floated through the window as Little Lu settled into her special painting chair and dipped her brush in the bluest blue. As her brush glided across the paper, a garden with bunnies and flowers appeared. She added bunches of carrots, trees, and clouds. Maybe a little more pink to accent the clouds...

"Wow Lu Lu, what a neat zoo picture! You really do have great paints. Do you think I could paint with you?"

A zoo picture? Little Lu leaned over and scowled. "Cousin Henry, can you just stay over there with the crayons? The strawberry crayon even smells a little like summertime. You'll love it!"

Little Lu continued with her creation, but Henry began bouncing the crayons on the table and then used them as drumsticks for a song he started to sing.

Little Lu stomped out of the room, straight to Mama. Certainly she would be able to fix this silly situation.

After Little Lu gave Mama her pile of frustrations, she stopped and waited. Hopefully Mama would tell Cousin Henry to go play outside. Instead Mama had a different idea.

"Lu Lu, helping Cousin Henry feel welcome means that you have to show him love."

"Oh I did, Mama. I put Cousin Henry in his very own spot with lots of crayons, away from me and my paints," Little Lu explained.

"Hmmm…. Love is hard, isn't it?" Mama answered, and Little Lu felt like she was changing the subject.

"Here is a poem that helps me remember what love looks like:

> *Let's start with this – you're important too.*
> *But when you're trying to love, it's not all about you."*

Little Lu listened and thought it was actually a nice little poem. She would try to use that poem with Cousin Henry. She sighed…. She knew what she had to do.

Little Lu walked back into the room and grabbed Cousin Henry's bag of books from the corner. His eyes brightened at the sight of them.

"Wow, are you going to read with me, Lu Lu?"

Cousin Henry found all of his favorite pages while talking very quickly and loudly. He was so excited! Little Lu pointed her head toward the book and tried to listen, but her eyes peeked up at her paints and the amazing garden painting she had created. She began to plan her next grand piece of art.

"Lu Lu...did you hear me? I said, what is your favorite part of this book?"

"Um..." Little Lu sighed again. This was not what she wanted to do. She wished the birds would start their art-time singing again.

Just then, Mama walked in and asked the two cousins how they were doing, sending a special glance toward Little Lu. But Little Lu just shrugged.

Mama knelt down and whispered sweetly in her ear,

"Let's start with this — you're important too.
But when you're trying to love, it's not all about you."

In such a short time, Little Lu had already forgotten that love poem.
She had tried, but it wasn't going very well. Little Lu decided she needed
to focus on that poem and try again with all her might.

Cousin Henry continued to turn the pages happily.
This time Little Lu really looked at the books.
Picture after picture, she eventually started to
notice how fun they were.

Her thoughts began to swirl. *Did a cheetah really
run with its legs wide like that? Crazy! A narwal is
just like a unicorn fish. How funny!*

Little Lu realized these books were too interesting to just look at and decided she should read the stories for Cousin Henry. Before they knew it, an hour of exciting reading had gone by. Soon they heard Cousin Henry's dad at the front door.

After giving Little Lu a huge hug, Cousin Henry ran outside, already telling his dad about all the fun they'd had.

Mama put her arm around Little Lu's shoulders and said, "Thank you for showing love today. Cousin Henry enjoyed the afternoon so much."

"Mama, I don't know if the love part actually worked. I did decide to look at the books with him instead of pretending. But then I started to enjoy the stories for myself too," Little Lu explained.

"I know you showed love today," Mama said. "Just like the poem says, you and the things you love are important. But when it's time to show love, it's okay to give thoughts about yourself a break for a bit while you really celebrate another person. Here's the best part — when you do that, you will often find yourself truly enjoying that other person."

Little Lu's eyes brightened. "This day has turned out to be fun after all! I even have some new ideas for my paintings!"

"And Mama? I like your poem, but I think we should add a second half:

Let's start with this — you're important too.
But when you're trying to love, it's not all about you.

Think just about you,
and you'll miss more than you know.
Celebrate another
and watch the real joy grow."

Hey Friend!

Little Lu is a dreamer too!

Have you ever had a day that felt like clouds and spicy onions?

Little Lu can relate! Being a kid isn't always easy, and each day has its own set of challenges. So what's a kid to do?

What about a little <u>dream</u> here and there? When Little Lu runs into a "bump in the road," she finds that her dreams and daydreams give her the spark and inspiration she needs to overcome obstacles in a new and creative way.

≷Spoiler alert≷
Dreams can even cause clothing adjustments...

Available on Amazon!
and
www.leahvisauthor.com

Made in the USA
Middletown, DE
16 February 2021